Choosing A Path

CHOOSING A PATH

By DAVID D. MOORE

AFRICAN AMERICAN IMAGES
CHICAGO, ILLINOIS

Illustrations by Harold Carr
First Edition, Third printing

DEDICATION

This book is dedicated
to my wife, Christie,
my mother, father, seven brothers
and to my yet unborn children.

I also dedicate this book
to all who will buy and read it,
and to my childhood friends,
who without realizing it
provided the inspiration
for my story.

ACKNOWLEDGEMENTS

Writing a book is usually a one-person task, but the inspiration behind it requires a sharing of experiences with several people. At least that was the case with this book and there are certain people, I personally want to thank.

Primarily, I thank my wife, Christie. Not only do I value her input but, more importantly, I cherish her support as a friend.

I am indebted to my mother-in-law, Dr. Wilesse Comissiong, who constantly provides me with invaluable support and information.

I know that this could not have been possible without the help of my grade school teachers, who taught me to read and write.

I would also like to thank my parents for making me do my homework over the years.

I would also like to give special thanks to my friends from the University of Massachusetts at Amherst, who worked with *Nummo News*. You gave me the opportunity to see my earlier writings in print and, through your inspiration, I am now writing books and plays.

Thanks to the brothers of my fraternity Alpha-Phi-Alpha.

I owe a special note of gratitude to Dr. Margaret Burnham for her much needed legal assistance.

A special mention goes out to African American Images for publishing my first book.

D.D.M.

It's Sunday morning and 10 year old Corey is waking from a long night's sleep. Corey can smell the aroma from his mother's breakfast. Corey knows that his mother will soon be coming up to his room to make sure that he is getting dressed for Sunday school. Corey sits up in his bed and wonders why his mother won't ever let him stay home, while she goes to Sunday school without him. But Corey knows better. Hearing his mother coming up the stairs, Corey stops daydreaming. As he hurriedly gets out of bed, he wipes his eyes and puts on his slippers.

Corey runs into the bathroom, turns on the water, and quickly jumps into the shower. He then quickly gets dressed and goes downstairs. Corey's mother (Mrs. Ann Haines) says to her son, "Corey what took you so long to come downstairs today?" "Mama, I was thinking how nice it would be if you went to church without me today. Then I could go out and play with Tyrone at the park." "Corey, first of all you know the house rules. If the Lord blesses us with another Sunday, we should thank him in His church. All you want to do Corey, is play. You don't want to listen when we tell you how important it is getting an education. Your daddy and I are going to make sure you finish high school and stay out of trouble. Secondly son, I told you not to play in that park. There is nothing but trouble down there. Just last night I heard a lot of loud talking, car doors slamming, and gunshots. All those youth do at that park is sell drugs and try to get kids like you hooked on that stuff.

Corey said, "Oh Mama come on, not that again!" "Corey don't tell me, 'Oh mama come on'. You children today think parents don't know what's going on out there. Well Corey I tell you we aren't stupid like you think we are. We formed a group last month called Parents Against Drugs. We meet every Wednesday, because we are sick and tired of worrying about our children every time we hear a police siren or every time we hear a gunshot. We're tired of going to the police station to get you children out of jail, or scraping to buy things for the house, because we're having to use that money for bail.

"Mama you know I don't get into trouble like that; you don't even let me play with everybody", says Corey. "But Corey don't you see why I have those rules for you and why I keep after you all the time? I love you Corey and your Daddy loves you too!" Just then Corey's dad (James Haines) comes downstairs. He says to his wife, "Ann I heard you preaching to Corey all the way upstairs in the bathroom. Why don't you leave the boy alone? He's a good child." "I know that James, but if we don't show Corey how much we care about him and how much we love him, he might not stay one." "Look at Corey's friend Tyrone, he could be a good boy too if his father was at home or if his mother spent time with him. Almost as soon as she gets home, she leaves again to go to a part-time job. So who is raising Tyrone? Corey told me last week that Tyrone doesn't have to go to Sunday school or church; therefore, Corey thinks Tyrone has it made." Ann stops pacing and says, "We have got to show Corey we care and let him know he can be anything he wants to be when he grows up. But Corey has to listen to us and know that we care for him."

Corey's father stirs uneasily in his chair and feels he can't get a word in edgewise. So he waits patiently until his wife is finished talking. Finally, Ann stops talking and James leans forward in his chair, places his hands on the table, "Ann, I know you're right, but you give Corey that same speech almost every week. Now let's stop talking and start eating so we can get out of here and go to church. I have to get to church early or Deacon Elder will take my seat."

As the family drives to church, Corey is sitting in the back seat. He notices his friend Tyrone outside playing. Corey yells to him, "I'll see you when I get back Tyrone!" and waves goodbye. Just a block from the church, Corey sees a group of older boys standing on the corner wearing Jordans and nice sweatsuits. Corey thinks they are lucky by not having to go to church, because they are almost grown. Corey's friend Tyrone sometimes hangs out with that group of older boys.

In church, Corey can't seem to sit still. He looks around the large sanctuary and hears the choir singing. He can see the deacons, male and female, sitting up front, nodding their heads when the Reverend speaks. The organ plays strongly in the background. The ushers are standing by the doors and in the aisles greeting church members and handing out programs. The deacons are in their clean white dresses and suits, as they prepare to serve communion. Corey's mother and father take communion, but pass the plate by Corey. He doesn't get communion yet, but he's used to that. Up front the Reverend says, "Now may we all share this Communion in remembrance of the Lord, Jesus Christ," then the congregation sings the songs of fellowship as they join hands and the last prayer is said. All the church members start milling about the church, talking church business and what they did since they last saw each other, and of course they talked about their children. People start shaking hands and filing out the back door of the church.

When Corey gets home, he rushes upstairs and changes his clothes to play outside with Tyrone. Corey looks out the window as he's changing his clothes and he sees Tyrone sitting on the front stairs of his house. Corey runs downstairs making lots of noise and yells out to his parents, "I'm going next door to play with Tyrone. I'll be back for dinner".

Corey dashes across the yard to meet with Tyrone. "How was church Corey?" "Same old thing, lots of singing, talking and people dressed up. You should come with us sometime Tyrone." "Maybe I will someday." But Corey knows better. They have the same conversation each week after church. "Hey Corey I've got something to show you!" Tyrone sounds real excited all of a sudden. "What you got Tyrone?" Tyrone looks around quickly like it's really a big secret. "Come to the side of the house, then I'll show you." "Tyrone, why can't you show me here?" "Corey you know your mother watches us from the window when we play. I don't think she wants you to be my friend and I don't want her to see the secret." So the two boys hurry over to the side of the house where Corey's mother can't see them. "Okay Tyrone, now show me the big secret!" Tyrone looks around again with a wide eyed look on his face. "First Corey you have to promise not to tell." Corey wonders what can the big secret be. He knew Tyrone liked to feel important and he always seemed to have all the answers to everything. Tyrone hardly ever makes him promise not to tell unless it's really something important. As the sun comes out from behind the clouds, Tyrone once again looks around with the same wide eyed look and then pulls out of his pocket a $100 dollar bill.

Corey's eyes pop open wide. "Where did you get all that money Tyrone!" "Be quiet Corey; don't talk so loud. Those big kids at the park gave it to me." "You mean they just gave it to you for nothing?"

Tyrone shakes his head, "No stupid, they were over there last night, and they called me over and said, 'Yo homey, we'll give you $100 if you stand out here and yell to us when the cops come'. You mean all I have to do is yell if the cops come? The biggest guy in the red sweatsuit said 'Yeah, that's all you have to do. Now do you want the money or not?' So Corey I told them, 'Of course I want the money.' That's how I got it, all while you were probably dead asleep."

"But Corey, I forgot to tell you, while the three guys

were in the building, I heard a lot of yelling and then a gunshot. Two of the big kids came out and the one in the red sweatsuit said, 'Hey don't run, walk slow and act natural so you don't attract any more attention.' After that, I ran home and hid under the bed until my mother came home." "Did you tell your mother what happened Tyrone?" "What, are you crazy?! My mother would kill me if she ever found out about that. When she's at work she thinks I'm in the house watching TV or something. And she always calls at 9 pm to check on me, so I go home at 8:45 pm, and wait until she calls, then I go back out again." "Weren't you scared Tyrone?" (Even though Corey knew Tyrone would lie and say he wasn't scared.) "No, I wasn't scared until I heard the gun. After that, I hid beside the bushes. When I heard the door open, I popped out." "That's what my mama was talking about when she heard police sirens last night, a lot of yelling and a gunshot," said Corey. Tyrone continued, "My mother heard on the radio this morning that somebody got killed over a drug deal. She said something about one of those men selling somebody some drugs that were fake."

"My mother and father don't let me go to that park. They tell me to stay away from there. They say its dangerous and I could get in trouble or killed. Last month, Johnny Washington got killed over there, just playing, and he was only 11 years old."

But Tyrone laughed, "I play over there all the time and nothing ever happens to me. I hear all the big guys talk. They say they make $5000 a week selling drugs. They drive nice cars and wear big gold rope chains, and have a lot of girls hanging around them all the time. One day I'm going to be like that too." But Corey looked at Tyrone close and said, "Tyrone do you really want to be like them?" Tyrone looked Corey straight in the eyes and said "Of course man, who wouldn't? They have it made. And they make more money than both your parents put together Corey! Besides, they are always nice to me. Yesterday, Vic the leader in the red sweatsuit said he might let me be a runner for them."

Corey had a puzzled look on his face and said, "Tyrone, I don't want to be like them. They all end up dead, in jail, or a junkie. Tyrone, what's a runner anyway?" Tyrone just shook his head like he always does when he knows something that Corey doesn't know. "Boy Corey, don't you know anything? You need to get out more, instead of always going home so early. Man you miss all the action." Corey cuts in, "Aw c'mon are you going to tell me or not?" Tyrone laughs and says, "All right, don't be so pushy. A runner is someone that brings the drugs and money to the dealer."

Tyrone then says, "Maybe I can move up in the gang and become a leader like Vic and have it made like he does." But Corey thought about it and said, "Tyrone aren't you afraid of getting mixed up in the drug life and one day going to jail or getting shot and maybe killed? Those guys always run when cops come around. Their life doesn't look so good to me. My mom and dad warn me all the time about it."

Tyrone snapped back, "Get with the times Corey. Your mom and dad don't know what they're talking about. Those guys have everything and they make it look easy. I hear them talk about it all the time. They say selling crack, heroine, PCP, and reefer is the easiest thing a Black man can do to get ahead. And they say as long as people want the stuff, they will always have a job. Sure, sometimes they get beat-up if a deal goes bad, or get shot at or some get killed, but they say that only happens to the stupid ones." "Yeah right. My folks said everybody in that line of business is stupid", snapped Corey. "I know someone who is so good, he can pay all the bills for his mother. Can you do that Corey?" Corey looked bewildered, "No Tyrone I can't, but my folks don't need help from drug money. When sirens sound, my parents don't get scared or look over their shoulder. When they go to work, they don't get beat-up or

shot at." "Well Corey, everybody isn't as lucky as your parents. It still looks good to me." Just then Corey heard his mother call him in for dinner. Corey told Tyrone he'd see him tomorrow at school. Corey walked home, got cleaned up, and then sat down for dinner.

Once Corey was seated, his mother and father said blessings over the meal. Corey's mother asked "What's wrong? You have a blank look on your face." But Corey just sat there daydreaming and playing with his fork. His mother asked again, "Corey what's wrong with you?" Corey slowly looked up raising his eyes and putting down the fork, "Oh nothing momma, I was just thinking". But Ann knew better. "Corey you better tell me what happened today while you were with Tyrone." Corey's dad said, "Corey start talking! You look funny to me too".

"I promised Tyrone I wouldn't tell." Corey's father raised his voice and said, "I don't care what you promised Tyrone. If you know what's good for you son, you'll start talking before you start hurting from my belt". So Corey told the whole story about the $100, Tyrone hanging around Vic and the rest of the drug dealers, and how Tyrone might get involved in helping the gang sell drugs.

Corey's father said, "You know better than to get involved with those drug dealers. You could end up in jail or dead before you even make any money. Those drug dealers aren't ever going to make anything of themselves. And each year they get younger and younger as the older ones get jailed or killed. So you see son, its just a vicious cycle and those kids selling that junk are just helping to keep African Americans down. They make sure that we never get a chance to improve our future. The white man will always provide you with drugs and jobs in the drug business. That kind of business may earn money for five or ten people in our community, but it's going to hurt 50-100 people in our community who will get hooked and want nothing but more drugs. Those youths don't have jobs that will earn them enough money to buy the drugs. Do you know how they earn their money?" Corey shook his head no to his father.

"Well I'll tell you then, most drug dealers start out young, let's say 12 years old or so. They start hanging around those drug dealers and end up first as lookouts while the dealers are committing a crime. But a dealer won't call it doing a crime, they will tell you they're just doing a job. But just like your friend Tyrone; last night he got paid $100. Tyrone doesn't even realize he could have gotten killed too, when they started shooting in that house. But to go on with how they get money, most kids steal money, tv's, stereos, jewelry, and other valuables from their parents and other relatives. You name it they steal it. Then they start stealing from neighbors, they steal bikes, cars, and so on. That's how they get the money; they steal, lie, cheat, and kill for it. It's also why they get scared when they hear sirens. Corey, that's the kind of lifestyle your mother and I are desperately trying to protect you from. If your friend Tyrone doesn't get more attention and help from his mother, he's going to end up in that dead-end cycle too."

"Do you understand what I'm saying to you and why I'm telling you all this?" Corey put his hands in his lap and shakes his head, "Yes dad, I understand". Corey's mother interrupts and says, "Come on, let's finish eating before the food gets cold. I'm going to tell Tyrone's mother about all this tomorrow."

After dinner, Corey's mom and dad continued talking about everything that Corey told them. They both agreed that they have a good son because they both put a lot of time, love, and care into Corey. They do things as a family with him. They also tell Corey how much they love him. The Haines know not all parents have that kind of relationship or dedication with their child. Some parents don't have that much concern or just can't seem to find the time. They both agreed to include Tyrone in their plans whenever possible and would try to get him to go to church with them on Sundays. The family goes to bed with thoughts of Corey and his friend Tyrone on their minds.

It's a new day; the birds are singing; the cars are rushing by; and people are on their way to work or school. Corey's parents are downstairs cooking breakfast. Corey's mother yells upstairs to wake Corey up and Corey rolls over in bed. Corey's father goes upstairs and pokes his head into the room and says, "Are you awake?" Corey sits up and answers, "Yes dad." "I'm on my way to work now, but I want you to come straight home from school today because you and I need a haircut. After work today I'll pick you up at the house." "OK dad, I'll come straight home after school. Can I get a hightop fade?" "Sure son, why not? I'll see you at 5:30. Have a good day at school."

Corey laid back down as soon as his father left and drifted back to sleep. He can barely hear in the background his father's car start up. He knows his father is on his way to another day at work. Corey's mother yells again, "Corey, you better get up, I have to go to work after you get dressed and fed". Corey finally rolls over, throws the covers off, stumbles over to the radio and bumps along the hallway to the shower.

After Corey got showered, he went downstairs, and ate breakfast. Corey's mother said to him, "You know Corey, I'm going to talk with Tyrone's mother today before I go to work, and I'm going to tell her everything we talked about last night". Corey got upset and shouted, "Mom if you tell Tyrone's mom everything, he won't trust me anymore and I'll lose my best friend. I promised Tyrone I wouldn't tell his secret!".

"I know you promised honey, but this is more important than a secret between two 10 year old children. We're talking about Tyrone's future and his mother has a right to know. You might not understand all this now honey, but it could save Tyrone's life. But baby, I promise you after all this is done, you and Tyrone will still be friends. This will blow over, you'll see".

Corey knew he was not going to change his mother's mind, so he grabbed his lunch and walked out the door to go to school. Corey thought as he walked, I'll be lucky if I don't bump into Tyrone today and then our friendship will last a little longer.

Corey wasn't even one block from his house when he spotted Tyrone talking with Vic and his gang of drug pushers in the park. Vic handed Tyrone a small brown bag, patted him on the back, and told him to run across the street and walk to school with Corey as they usually do.

Tyrone and Corey walked in silence for a whole block. Corey finally asked, "What's in the bag that Vic gave to you?" "I knew you were going to ask me that. Vic gave me something that's going to help me start my own business." Corey stopped walking and looked at Tyrone with a surprised look on his face, "Tyrone are you crazy?" Do you know what you're getting yourself into? Don't you hear the cops and the ambulance come into our neighborhood almost every night? Don't you see the dealers and innocent bystanders getting shot-up and sometimes killed in those drive-by shoot-outs?" Tyrone calmly said, "Man are you finished? You sound like my mother. Just chill man. I know what I'm doing. I'm getting into the big time. I'm going to be big around here one day. I'm going to start dealing, for Vic, to the kids during school and after school. Vic's going to drive me to other neighborhoods in his BMW to show me the ropes and help me establish my own territory. Man I might even have you working for me one of these days. That is, if you ever wake up and figure out what time it is. I'm lucky to get such an early start. Most guys don't get started until they're 12 or 13. I'm still 10. I could be a kingpin by 15 and have my own BMW and jewelry, and of course babes."

"Man I'm worried about you. You've changed a lot.

Right now you don't do drugs or at least I don't think you do. But you can't hang around all that dealing and crime and not get hooked and probably arrested or killed. What if somebody beats you up one day, while you're selling or worse, shoots you and takes your money and drugs? What will your mother have to say about your new life?"

Tyrone stopped walking and turned around quickly to Corey and said, "Man funny thing you brought up my mother. Last night after you and I finished playing she sat me down and started talking about how I've been hanging out at the park with Vic and those guys. She told me she doesn't want me playing in the park anymore. She said she's going to talk with your parents to see if we could catch a ride with them and start going to church with you. Later on that night, I could hear her on the phone talking to my grandmother in North Carolina. She was telling grandma stuff like, 'I just don't know what I'm going to do with that boy. He just won't listen to me. He acts like he can't hear me when I'm trying to discipline him.' She also said, I'm always in trouble and my grades are slipping and that I started skipping school."

"She told my grandma that if I don't start doing better by the end of the school year, she's going to send me to North Carolina because she doesn't have the time right now to give me what I need. She didn't think I could hear her on the phone, but I was right at the top of the stairs and heard every word my mother said. Man I don't want to go to North Carolina to live with my grandparents. That's where mostly all of the older people in my family are and they're boring. There's no excitement there. I'm just about to get my business started and things are just starting to happen for me here."

"Man how are you going to keep drug dealing hidden from your mother?" "You sure have a lot of questions and what ifs. First of all, you need to stop calling it drugs and crime. We like to call it a business. We sell happiness not drugs. We just give people what they want. It's the way to get ahead now days. You don't have to do a 9 to 5 anymore if you don't want to, that's for suckers and I'm too young to work at McD's. Let's keep walking, I've got to get to school and open my business today. It's my first day on the job you know. I want to do good and make Vic proud." Corey just shakes his head, "You don't know what you're getting yourself into". "Like I said man, you don't know what time it is. Let's get into school and stop arguing. I get enough of that at home from my mother."

As the school day goes on, Tyrone makes a few connections in the hallways and the locker room at gym. The students at school are stepping up to buy into a slow death, not knowing that Tyrone and others like him are throwing their lives away because drugs will lead them to nowhere. But most youth have to learn the hard way.

The school bell rings and Corey runs out the door with the rest of his classmates. As Corey walks to the front of the school, students are standing around Vic's red BMW and Tyrone is sitting in the car with Vic while the car stereo is blasting. As Tyrone makes his last sale on school grounds for the day, the engine starts and Corey sees Tyrone hand Vic the money as he walks by. Corey doesn't walk up to the car or hang around like the others that envy Vic, and now Tyrone. Corey starts walking home alone.

Corey opens the front door to his house, hangs up his coat, walks over to the refrigerator and makes himself a sandwich. As he sits down he starts to think about his friend and his new lifestyle. He thinks for a while and then starts doing his homework. Later, He turns on the TV and watches the Cosby show. As soon as the Cosby show goes off, Corey's father drives up into the yard. Mr. Haines enters the room and asks, "Corey how was school today?" "It was fine dad; I walked to school with Tyrone today so I guess mom didn't talk with Ms. Woods yet." "Don't you worry about that son. You and Tyrone will still be friends

when this is all over. I have to go upstairs to change my clothes. When I come back down we can go to the barber shop." Mr. Haines turns around and starts going up the stairs as Corey sits back down to watch TV.

Only 10 minutes go by and Corey can hear his father coming down the stairs. His father says, "Corey are you ready?" Corey puts on his coat, "I'm ready dad". "When we get back, your mother will be going to the *Parents Against Drugs* meeting after we have dinner." They both walk out the door to the car.

As they ride, Corey tells his father that there's a play next week being performed at the Paul Robeson Center by the 'Black Theatre Production' called, 'Malcolm X', that his teacher would like for the students to see. "Can you and Mom take me?"

"I'll have to speak to your mother about it Corey before I can answer that, because we're both busy and I don't want to say yes and later on let you down. What day is the play next week?"

"It's on Wednesday night dad." "Okay after I speak with your mother, we'll both let you know." They drive up to the barber shop, get out of the car, and walk into the shop. As they enter the shop, they see only two customers waiting. "Looks like we got lucky Corey, we must have missed the crowd." Mr. Jameson turns around from cutting a customer's hair and says "Come on in you two, I haven't seen you in awhile. Have a seat, it shouldn't be long before I get to you."

Mr Jameson asked Mr. Haines, "James what did you think of that Lakers/Celtics game on TV last night?" "That game was a shocker. It was the most exciting game that I've seen in a few years. I thought the Lakers were going to lose. I wanted to drive to the Boston Garden last night, but the family spent the day and evening at church.

"James, what about the play all the youth are talking

about on Malcolm X?" "Corey was just telling me about it and said he doesn't want to miss it." "That's all my two sons have been talking about the last few days is that Malcolm X play. It seems like if I don't take them I better not come home." Corey's face lit up when they started talking about the Malcolm X play. "So dad are we going?" "Corey as we discussed in the car, I'll let you know after I talk to your mother about it."

Just then Mr. Jameson said, "All right, which one of you is going first?" Corey said, "I will" and he looks at his father as Mr. Haines nods his approval. Corey hops up into the chair and gets comfortable. Mr. Jameson picks up the cloth and drapes it over Corey and pins it up in the back. "Well young man what can I do for you today?" "I want a hightop fade with a part." Mr. Jameson looks at Mr. Haines and he nods his approval. The clippers turn on and Mr. Jameson goes to work as Corey's father picks up the latest edition of the Final Call newspaper and starts reading.

After 10 minutes go by its time for Mr. Haines to sit in the chair as Corey reads the 'Jet' magazine. Mr. Jameson finishes with Mr. Haines' haircut and the money is exchanged. Mr. Jameson gives the change back and Corey puts on his coat. Mr. Jameson says, "I'll see you two in a few weeks". Corey and his father walk out the door and get into the car.

Soon after they're home, Corey's mother comes into the room, sits down, and says "Hello Corey, how was school today?" Corey looks up,"It was okay mom. Did you talk with Ms. Woods yet?" "Are you still worried about that? Well yes, while you and your father were at the barber I went next door and spoke with Ms. Woods." Corey then looked down,"So that means I don't have a best friend anymore." Mrs. Haines said, When I left she was calling Tyrone into the room to talk with him. Corey you'll see this will be over soon and you and Tyrone will be best friends again like nothing ever happened. So come on, lets get

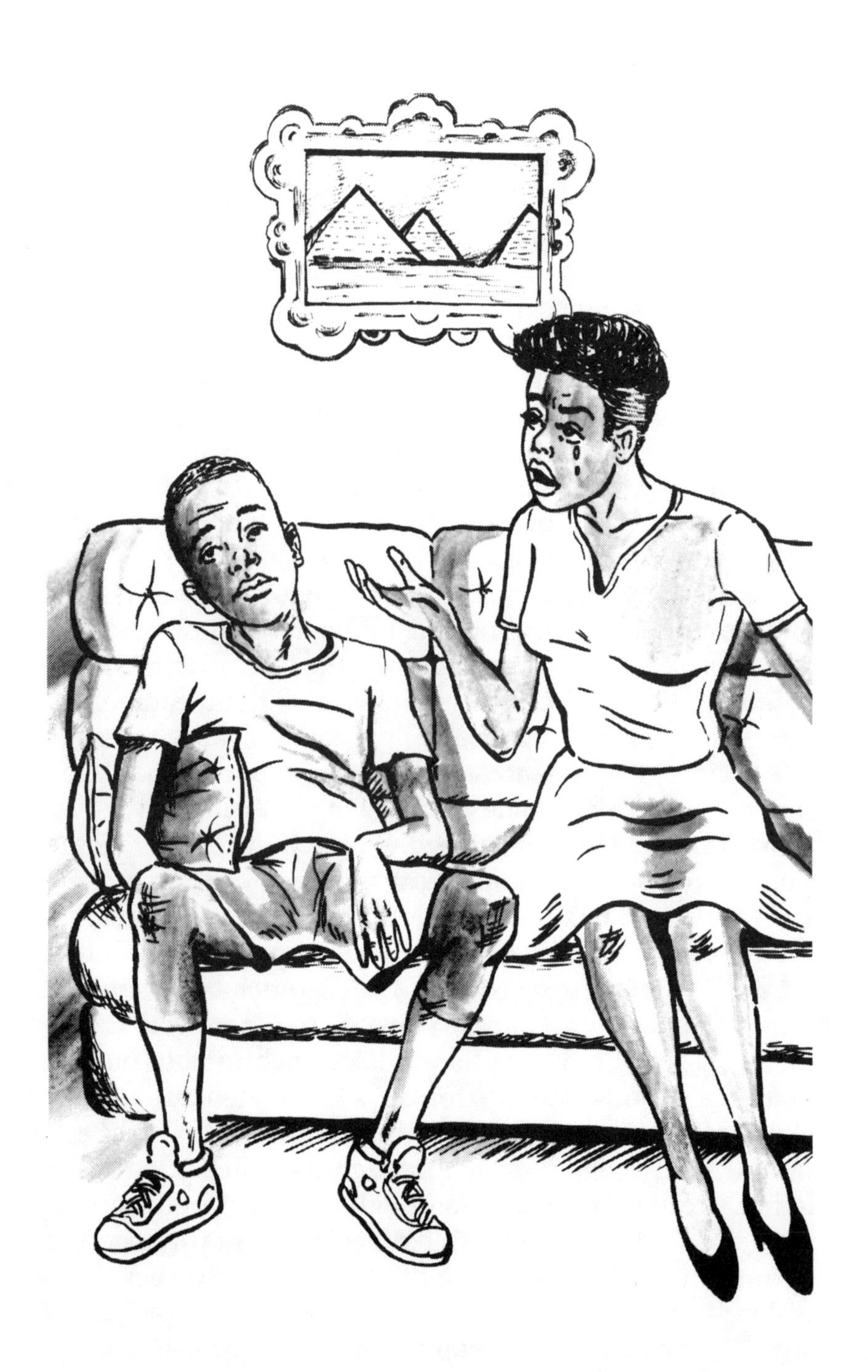

ready for dinner. After dinner I'm going to the *Parent Against Drugs* (PAD) meeting at the church." The Haines family sat down to dinner and Mr. Haines blessed the food. After dinner Mrs. Haines put on her coat and drove to the church to the (PAD) meeting.

Meanwhile, next door Tyrone and his mother, Veronica, were having their talk about Sunday's events and the $100. Tyrone's mother said, "Sit down, I want to talk with you." Tyrone tried to look like he had no idea what his mother wanted. But he was able to hear parts of the conversation between his mother and Mrs. Haines from his room. Tyrone knew this was going to be a long talk. So he slowly dragged into the room wearing his best puzzled look and reluctantly sat down.

"I just had a talk with Mrs. Haines and she told me about you hanging around that park after I told you not to, and about how you could have gotten killed being a lookout for those boys that sell drugs in that park. Now they've got you selling drugs for them." "Mama I wasn't in any danger the other night." Ms. Woods slammed her hand down hard on the table and yelled at Tyrone and said, "Tyrone don't interrupt me when I'm talking to you. You're only 10 years old, you don't know everything."

Ms. Woods continued, "I don't know what's been going on in your head lately, if you keep hanging out with that crowd that sells drugs you'll end up just like them, or worse. You are too young to throw your life away. Son, I love you and it might not seem like much to you, but I'm doing all I can to provide for us. I know it seems like I'm always at work, but the bills have to be paid or we'll be put out on the streets. I know its rough for you not having a father around and its also rough on me not having a husband around. But we can both get through this together if we help each other and be honest with each other. "

"Tyrone, outside of our relatives in North Carolina you are all I have. I know the Haines family next door has been very nice to us, but we have to stick together, son. I can't be with you every minute of the day. If I could do that, I gladly would and there is nothing I'd rather do than be with you. Do you understand what I'm saying to you son?" Tyrone nodded his head yes while half crying. Ms. Woods then said, "But I need the two jobs I've got so that we can have a home. You might not understand that until you get older or have a wife and child of your own. Tyrone, I need you to help me." Tyrone started shifting in his chair and sat straight up. He had never heard his mother tell him, 'I need you to help me' before. Ms. Woods continued, "Tyrone I need you to be a responsible young man while I'm at work. I already have so many worries and pressures. I don't want to be at work worrying about if you're at home or out in the streets. I spoke to your grandmother last night and I told her that if you don't get better grades and start acting right, I'm going to send you to her for a while until you are ready to come back. I don't want to do that, but the choice is yours. I want you to know the conditions that I'm laying out to you. You either start doing better in school and stay away from those drug dealers in that park or you'll soon be going to North Carolina. You will be choosing your own path son. How you do in the next two or three months will tell the story".

"So Tyrone, I'm going to be watching you closely and talking with the Haines family and in the next two months, I will decide if you stay here or go away to be with your grandparents." "Do you understand everything I've said to you?" "Yes mom, I understand. I won't hang out at the park anymore or deal drugs for Vic's group." But Tyrone knew he was lying to his mother. Ms. Woods said, "Okay as long as we understand each other you can go wash your hands and we'll have dinner".

At the same time Mrs. Haines is at the church attending the (PAD) meeting with 12 other parents. The meeting is called to order. A story is told by the founders, Mr. and

Mrs. Robinson, to the four new members present about how their son was shot while a local drug dealer was making a sale to him. "We started going around and knocking on doors to find out how many parents would be interested in forming a group that would try to take back the streets and reclaim the lives of our children. It took a few months before we could carve out a strategy."

Mrs. Robinson continued, "But after much talking and planning we decided it was time to reach out to the community. That is why many of you are here tonight. As parents, we decided that we can patrol the park to try to get those dealers to move out of our community. Secondly, you can help by recording license plate numbers and turning them in to the police. We can also let the police know at what time the dealers are most active and how many people are involved."

Mr. Robinson stepped forward and said, "Now we'd like to turn the meeting over to any parents that might have questions." Mr. Brown (one of the new members) stood up and asked, "What can we do about these youth that get arrested and before the week is out you see them right back in the park as if they only had to pay a parking ticket?" Mr. Robinson answered, "I understand your concern, at the next meeting we will invite the police chief, a judge, and a lawyer to address this issue." Mrs. Douglas (another new member) stood up and said, "I don't like all the foul language and trash they bring into the neighborhood. They throw beer bottles, paper bags, and write graffiti all over the place. Our children think those dealers are the coolest dudes they know. I'm worried about the role model image those dealers are becoming." Mrs. Robinson replied, "If we continue to get help from parents who live in the community, we can change that. If we keep watch, keep our kids away from that park, and bring our kids into the house at a certain time, those dealers won't have anyone to peddle that mess to. We must become the role models, and provide recreational and employment opportunities.

Mrs. Haines stood up and said, "A 10 year old child that lives next door to me started selling drugs for those dealers and he's selling it in the schools now. They don't care what age the child is; they just recruit to get their dirty work done." Several parents responded in agreement.

Mrs. Robinson urged the group to calm down. After the room was quiet again, Mrs. Robinson announced, "The watch in the park will begin tomorrow and we need volunteers. We need you to sign up tonight. We already have picket signs made up. We also want all of you to wear these sweatshirts so we can be identified as members of the group. That way other parents watching might want to join and they'll know who they need to contact. Now, if you want to take action to end the fear please sign the board before leaving." Mr. Robinson asked, "Are there any more questions or suggestions?" One parent stood up and asked, Will the Reverend be there?" Mr. Robinson answered,"Yes the Rev. will be there. So lets close out the meeting in prayer and we'll then sign up before we leave the church." After the prayer, the parents signed up on the board and agreed to go home and call other parents to see if they wanted to volunteer for duties in the park. The parents left the church excited. They are going to start taking control, instead of feeling helpless.

The morning came quickly, Tyrone heard his mother calling upstairs to wake him up. Ms. Woods yelled, "Tyrone your breakfast is on the table, so hurry up, get dressed, and eat,so you and Corey can walk to school." Tyrone sat up in his bed and thought, walk to school with Corey? She must be crazy. I'm not even his friend anymore. Ms. Woods yelled again, "Tyrone don't let your food get cold. I have to catch my bus. I have to go now, but I'll see you when I get home. Have a nice day at school and remember what we talked about last night. I love you!" Just then the door slammed and Ms. Woods ran down the block to catch her bus.

Tyrone got out of bed and wondered how he was going to get out of walking to school with Corey. Tyrone showered quickly, got dressed and ran downstairs to eat breakfast. Just as he put the plate into the sink he heard the beep of a car horn outside. He pulled the curtain aside and looked out the window. He saw Vic's red BMW parked in front of the house. Tyrone hurried to put on his coat and rushed out to the car. Tyrone hopped into the car and said to Vic, "I didn't expect you". "I know but I've got to look out for my number one junior salesman". Vic handed Tyrone a shopping bag, "Look in the bag. I got a few gifts for you." Tyrone looked into the bag and his eyes popped open as he sat beaming with pride. Tyrone yelled, "You mean you bought these for me?" "Of course. You did real good on your first day. So I bought you some new pump tennis shoes and a Michael Jordan sweatsuit. We've got to have our people looking good as they conduct business." Tyrone grabbed the sneakers out of the bag, took off his old shoes, and tossed them out the window as he put on the new shoes. "They fit perfect too. How did you know?" "Man don't you know? Vic knows all." But Vic didn't tell Tyrone that all the gifts he gave Tyrone were stolen from stores by his gang members. He let Tyrone think that he paid for the gifts out of his pocket. Vic started up the car, turned around and headed in the direction of the school.

While next door at Corey's home, Corey was watching out of his front window as Tyrone ran to get into Vic's car. Corey knew that Tyrone must know that he told the secret. Corey was a little sad and felt that he had lost his best friend. He thought, "Well I guess I'll be walking to school by myself from now on." Corey left the house to start walking alone.

Later on in the day at the school, Tyrone was standing at his locker. He had on the new sweatsuit and sneakers, and told the other students approaching him how he got them as a gift from Vic. The other classmates envied

501

Tyrone. They started to hand Tyrone the money when Tyrone yelled out, "Traitor!" Corey stopped walking and wondered if he should try to explain, but he kept walking and figured it was no use. The days went by. Tyrone kept selling drugs, Corey continued walking to school alone, and they still weren't speaking to each other. Corey missed his friend and wondered if Tyrone missed the friendship they once had. Corey noticed that Tyrone was dressing better. He now had a lot of spending money to impress the other children.

At lunch time, Corey sat alone. Tyrone sat at the table with a new group of admiring friends. Tyrone was telling them stories about Vic driving him around to different neighborhoods and how he sells drugs and makes lots of money. The other classmates now look up to Tyrone. As the school day ends, Corey walks home alone again.

When Corey got home he put down his books and turned on the TV. An hour later, he heard gun shots and minutes later a loud pitch siren of an ambulance and police cars a few blocks away. Corey continued to watch the Cosby show. He had no idea that the sirens were coming to pick up his friend Tyrone because he got shot twice in the leg in a drive-by shooting from a rival drug gang. A few blocks away Tyrone was squirming on the ground and feeling incredible pain through his whole body, and he was screaming. The warm flow of blood was running down his leg, soaking his pants in a matter of seconds. Vic and his gang don't even ask Tyrone if he's okay; they just turned and ran in different directions before the police arrive. As the ambulance arrives with the police shortly behind, Tyrone is the only person left in the park as a few onlookers just start crossing the streets to see what has happened.

Just then Corey's parents drive into the driveway. After entering the house they tell Corey they saw Tyrone being lifted into the ambulance in front of the park. A loud scream is heard and they know it's Tyrone's mother, Ms. Woods.

Seconds later, a loud knock on the door is heard. Mrs. Haines opens the door and Ms. Woods is hysterically screaming, but manages to ask for a ride to the hospital. They all jump into the car and speed off to the hospital. It seems that before the car doors all slam, Ms. Woods is already checking in at the emergency room to see Tyrone.

As the other three check in at the desk, Ms. Woods is pacing the floor and saying, "Please Lord let my baby be all right" over and over again. So they all wait for news as the doctor and nurses are treating Tyrone's wounded leg. Corey's family and Ms. Woods gaze around the room at the families and other people waiting to be seen by the doctors and staff. Another mother cries out and says, "No, not my baby. Not my child!".

One little girl is still in her chair not understanding what's going on as she plays with her doll. The siren of an ambulance pulls up and another drug related patient is wheeled into the hospital. At the same instant, the head nurse walked into the waiting room with her cleanly pressed white nurse's outfit seeming to shine and asked for the family of Tyrone Woods. Tyrone's mother jumped out of her chair with a wild look of anticipation in her eyes. She shouted, "Is my Tyrone all right?! Is he going to be okay, oh please tell me he's not dead! Not my child, not my baby!"

Nurse Jones looked Ms. Woods in the eyes, took her hand, and told her, "Yes, Tyrone is going to be all right. His wounds will heal in time, and he should be released in a week. You may go up and see him now." Ms. Woods said, "Thank you, thank you, oh thank you Lord!"

Corey's mother hugged Ms. Woods and told her they would wait downstairs as long as she liked. Ms. Woods answered, "Thank you for being so nice to me and being here with me when I needed you". Then Ms. Woods turned quickly and ran to the elevator to be with her son. She thought it took the elevator an eternity to come down. Finally the bell rang and she sprang onto the elevator and pushed the button for the fourth floor. The elevator door opened, she jumped out, passed the nurse's station, passed the restroom, and finally ran into room 431 to Tyrone's bedside, with tears streaming heavily down her cheeks.

She got to Tyrone's bedside crying and grabbed him up into her arms and cradled him as her tears fell onto Tyrone's neck. Ms. Woods said over and over again, "Oh Tyrone, thank God, baby you're all right." After a few minutes she sat down in a chair close to the bed and Tyrone told her he was sorry about lying to her and not staying away from the park and he's not selling drugs for Vic anymore. Ms. Woods started talking with Tyrone about how she told him to stay away from the playground and Vic's gang of drug dealers. She told Tyrone not to go back to that park or he would be going to North Carolina real soon.

After a few minutes, Ms. Woods told Tyrone, "I got a promotion and won't have to work two jobs anymore. I can spend more time with you now. I love you so much, and I always wondered about what you were doing while I'm at work and not able to watch you as closely as I should. I was really hoping this promotion would come through and I wouldn't have to slave to be able to buy things that you deserve and trying to keep a roof over our heads."

Ms.` Woods continued, "Tyrone you don't have any idea how hard it is for a woman out there trying to raise a child all by herself. It's no place for a child to be, out there, hustling drugs for some no good dealers. They will just use you and go on to someone else after they use you up or you get arrested or killed. They don't care anything about you."

Ms. Woods continued, "If I didn't know any better I would swear that animals like Vic prey on kids to sell drugs. It seems like they are trying to take over the world. That's not the way it's supposed to be. " Tyrone nodded his head and agreed not to go near the park anymore or work for Vic selling drugs. Ms. Woods said, "Tyrone, I heard all this before". "Honest mom, this time I mean it; after this, I won't go near that park or drugs ever again. I learned my lesson the hard way." Mom , I now see that it could have been worse." Just then Corey and his family walked into the room to visit Tyrone. Corey dashed to Tyrone's bedside, "Are you okay?" Tyrone smiled and answered, "Yes Corey I'm okay. Corey, are we still friends after the way I acted?" Corey smiled, "I sure hope so Tyrone, I missed playing with you and walking to school with you. It hasn't been the same since we stopped speaking to each other."

"Were you scared when you heard the shots and knew you were hit?" Tyrone just shook his head like he usually did when Corey doesn't know something. "Of course I was scared and the pain was 50 times worse than a toothache. I'm never going to the park again and I'm going to be good like you Corey." Ms. Woods smiled and said, "You don't have a choice Tyrone." At that instant the doctor came into the room to check on Tyrone and announced visiting hours were over and they would all have to leave.

Tyrone's mother hugged and kissed him and told him, "I love you Tyrone. I'll be back tomorrow as soon as visiting hours start. You get a good night sleep and call if you need anything or want to talk and don't give the doctors or nurses any trouble." As the families turned to walk out together Tyrone yelled to Corey, "When I get out I'll start going to church with you!" Corey turned, nodded his head and smiled. Ms. Woods said "We'll both start going to church". And the families embraced in a group hug before turning to leave.

Questions for Thought

1. Why did Vic recruit Tyrone rather than Corey?

2. Are you more like Tyrone or Corey?

3. List all your friends in two categories, those who act like Tyrone and those who act like Corey.

TYRONE	COREY

4. Which category do you fit into?

5. Why didn't Vic stay when Tyrone was shot?

6. How many drug dealers do you know?

7. What is the future like for drug dealers?

8. What do you think about Parents Against Drugs (PAD)?

9. What else can parents and the community do?

10. Have you ever been confronted by a drug dealer or a gang member?

11. What was your reaction?